Magnolia, Magnolia, Where Are You?

By Hubert Green

From the Heart

*

Printed in United States

2012 Re-Release

ISBN – 13: 978-1479390762

ISBN – 10: 1479390763

Published by: CreateSpace - Amazon

Thanks

I would like to thank the following
people: my daughter Tenell K. Green,
my neice Villette Waiters, my sister Viola
Waiters, my editors Terri Dingle and Deb-
orah Hughes, Yvonne Gray. Without the
help of these "Magnolias" I would not
have been able to complete this book.

Cover designer by Hubert Green

(To see the individuals in these stories go to web site below)

www.magnoliaworks.net

Preface

How Strong is your Friendship?

To what extent would you go to find a true friend?

Anna, a blue-eyed blond headed girl was born and raised in Africa. She lived near Sunamite, one of 12 African children. Sunamite's name was changed to Ebony when she reached South Carolina.

The two girls were separated through no choice of their own.

The beautiful Magnolia tree plays a big part in their lives. After you read this book, notice how the Magnolia Tree will become more noticeable to you in your everyday life, especially if you live in the South.

The last part of this book is a true story of how 12 Children remember my mother's love as they grew up on a Sharecropper's farm in Lynchburg, SC from the 1930s to the 1960s.

- Hubert Green

Contents

Part 1

Part 2

**A Sharecropper's Family (My family true story)
Page 65**

Part 3

Conclusion

Page 96

The Beginning

Could big things come from small beginnings? Well let's see. The tiny atom, if used in a certain way, can have explosive consequences. Our awesome universe no doubt had a beginning. "The diameter of our galaxy spans so vast a distance that if you could travel as fast as the speed of light (186,282 miles a second) it would take you 100,000 years to cross it! How many miles is that? Well, since light travels about six trillion (6,000,000,000,000) miles in a year, multiply that by 100,000 and you have the answer: our Milky Way galaxy is about 600 quadrillion (600,000,000,000,000,000) miles in diameter! The average distance between stars within the galaxy is said to be about six light-years, or about 36 trillion miles." This is a quote from a well-known book.

But can big things come from small beginnings? from small cities or towns? Consider Bethlehem, who came from that small town? Jesus was born there. In the Bible book of Micah it states at the 5th chapter verse 2, "And you, O Bethlehem Ephrathah, the one too little to get to be among the thousands of Judah, from you there will come out to me the one who is to become ruler in Israel, whose origin is from early times, from the days of time indefinite." Yes, today all the events in the world could not compare to the greatness of that event in connection with Jesus.

Part 1

Chapter 1

Magnolia

Magnolia, Magnolia, where are you? No city has just one Magnolia. We might speak of her in terms of a single Magnolia tree or as an individual. We have to identify her as a woman, either younger or older. Just like the beautiful Magnolia tree itself, evergreen, it is strong in comparison with other trees. It is able to withstand strong winds, drought, cold, and floods. The South, with her Magnolias, will be concentrated on in this book.

As you travel through the streets of Southern towns, you cannot but help to see the beautiful Magnolia trees. These trees are so beautiful, especially during the springtime of the year. What beautiful flowers are on those trees! They grow tall, short, and wide. Limbs touch the ground at times. In one town in South Carolina, called Florence, I would ride down the

Streets and say to myself, "Magnolia, Magnolia, where are you?" Then as I'd drive while silently counting to ten, a tree would show up before I could finish counting. That's how many Magnolia trees are in that town. Then I'd travel through the countryside and I'd see the same effect. I would count, and then a tree would be in someone's yard. Try it! In Florence, there is even a shopping center named the Magnolia Mall.

Let's look at the women, Magnolia's if you will, that have helped make southern families what they are. It is so easy to forget how much a mother, a daughter, a sister, an aunt, a niece, a daughter in-law, a mother in-law, a sister in-law, can be in a family. We could easily take them for granted. Just as we ride down the roads and streets and do not even recognize these beautiful Magnolia trees, we could easily take these individuals for granted. Keeping in mind that no one is perfect, we owe a great deal to the women in our lives!

Magnolias are located all over the world! Can you recognize them? I have found that in about every town there is a street that is named Magnolia. many, many pictures of Magnolia flowers grace wall after wall in homes and business I have visited. Even the little town that I am writing this book from, Lynchburg, South Carolina, was once named Magnolia, as you will see as you continue reading.

As was mentioned earlier, it is easy to forget the role these women played in the early history of our lives. In this book we will look back at life surrounding the history of South Carolina. Your history may be in another town, city, state or country. Wherever it may be, let's not take the roles these women play in our lives for granted.

Chapter 2

Sharecropper

I want to draw attention to a group of people that have been almost forgotten in this twenty-first century. They are the sharecroppers. I noticed that not much had been said about sharecroppers until I started e-mailing people and asking, "Why not?" Now books are showing up.

Sharecroppers are dying out with little or no recognition. I can write about this with some authority, because I am the seventh son of a sharecropper. There are many of us out there. If you meet someone from the South that's about 60 years old, he can tell you a story or two about what he went through as a sharecropper.

The women are given much attention because of their determination to support their husbands and love their family. They worked the fields beside their husbands while cooking, cleaning, bearing children, and caring for the sick. There were many times that they did all of the doctoring. The home remedies would come in good: sap from pine trees, the sassafras roots from the woods, and many other things.

The stories I am about to relate are not to incite hatred, but to show how, despite difficult times, some Magnolias touched their lives and helped them to be stronger individuals. Maybe these stories will encourage someone to not give up in doing what is good, right, kind, and loving.

Yes, this July 4th morning there is a true story that needs to be told about life in a small little town by the name of Lynchburg. It is located in South Carolina.

Though small, it is rich in examples of family caring and love. This story will focus on a sharecropper's family between the 1930s and 1960s. But, before the sharecropper's true story, I will tell you a fictitious story that begins in Africa in the late 1800s. If you want to go directly to the sharecropper's story then start reading on page 65. Otherwise continue reading and just image how it could have been for two close friends in Africa.

Chapter 3

Sunamite

Now just imagine a 16 years old young lady in West African sitting under a beautiful Magnolia tree. Her name is Sunamite. (Sun-a-mite) Her father Razier gave her that name because of her darker complexion. She is the youngest of 12 children, 7 boys and 5 girls. Her joy is being outside watching the animals, birds and the rest of God's creation.

It's mid-summer during the 1850s. Sunamite is just looking across the field of green grass with the background of dark green trees. The sound of birds singing all around her makes the day seems even better. The birds singing is never out of tune. Then – there they are again – the elephants are down at the large lake getting their daily drink of water. The lions' voices too, echo off the tall jungle trees. They are letting man and beast know whose territory they are in. The air is ever so fresh and clear. Maybe it is in part because of the large waterfall just a few miles away. Its rumbling can be heard at times.

The beauty that surrounds Sunamite's world can hardly be described. It looks like the Garden of Eden.

Very few outsiders have been able to find this remote part of the jungle. Her mother Nolia is in their hut taking care of her other children. There are many. Sunamite smells the aroma of the food her mother is cooking. She doesn't have a care in the world. Her father is off hunting game, along with some of her brothers. She knows her father never comes home without something to eat, even if it's a bird that he has killed for the meal. She feels the wind blowing across the field, ever so gentle. It catches her hair as it blows from one side to the other.

Sunamite has friends in the nearby villages who come by at times. One is of the white race. Her name is Anna. Anna's name means "one of grace." Anna's father, Mr. Trader comes by about once a month to buy goods from Sunamite's father Razier and other villagers. Sunamite's father is 40 years old. The villagers says Mr. Trader's name really suits him because he buys and trades goods. It is funny how his real name happens to be Mr. Trader.

How did Mr. Trader and Anna come to live in Africa? Well, one day after a bad storm occurred off the coast of West Africa, Razier and his sons went down to the shore to see what the storm had washed up. They always do this after a large storm. It always seems to be a very clear day after a bad storm passes. There, lying on the beach are a man and a woman. (Mr. Trader and his wife Sarah) They had floated in on a piece of the ship and some strange looking trees that Mr. Trader had tied together to help them float on the water. Razier had never seen trees like that before. The trees that Mr. Trader had tied together, while in the water to help them float, were Magnolia trees. Sarah had fallen in love with these trees. She wanted to take some of the trees to her mother that lived in Jerusalem to see if they would live. The ship was heading toward South Africa and then eventually to Jerusalem, Sarah's home.

She had not seen her family for 10 years. The trip was cut short by this huge hurricane that came off the West Coast of Africa. Everyone else on the ship of 70 persons lost their lives. Only Mr. Trader and Sarah survived. The ship was coming from Mr. Trader's home state of South Carolina, North America. He had promised Sarah he would take her back to see her parents if the crops did well that year. He worked with his brother on the farm.

The fields had a double crop that year. He wanted to keep his word. He loved his wife very much. Mr. Trader and Sarah would do everything together it seemed like. They would fish in the large lake, go swimming at the beach, and even hunt game together at times. They were best of friends. Mr. Trader had blonde hair and blue eyes. Sarah his wife had dark hair and darker skin than Mr. Trader.

Razier and his family cared for Mr. Trader and Sarah for months after the shipping accident. They liked Razier's family so much that after they continued their trip to see Sarah's parents, they wanted to re- turn to Africa and start their own trading business near Raziers village. Sarah gave Nolia two Magnolia trees. They planted the smallest one near the village and the largest one on the bank of the running river that lead to the waterfall. At this time neither Anna nor Sunamite were even born.

After a short period of time in West Africa Mr. Trader and Sarah continued their trip to Jerusalem.

Years went by, then Mr. Trade and Sarah returned

to West Africa to make it their home also.

About a year went by then, Anna a sky blue eye blonde hair girl was born to Mr. Trader and Sarah. She was the joy of their lives.

Then about 9 month later Nolia and Razier had their little smiling girl Sunamite (Sun-a-mite). There brown eyes bundle of joy.

Sunamite had been friends with Anna ever since they were old enough to walk. Sunamite's father took her with him when he went over to Anna's father house to buy items that they needed. Really, Sunamite does not need any other children to play with. Her mother and father have 12 children. Her mother is only 41 years old. Some of the children have already left to start their families in other villages. Sunamite is the youngest of five girls and seven boys. Nolia has taught her well. She can cook and clean as well as baby-sit some of the other villager's children.

Her brothers are known in the village as the best team of kick ball players. There were so many of them on the team nobody could beat them at this game. They were also the fastest swimmers and runners in the village.

Her mother had a set of twin boys. Their names were Sonrise and Sonset.

The reason Nolia named one Sonrise is because he was born at sunrise and he had eyes wide open shortly after birth. Sonset was named that because it seemed like to Nolia that the sun was setting before he was born. His eyes were closed when he was born. They are identical twins. About the only way you can identify them is, Sonrise keeps his eyes open wide, while Sonset has eyes partly closed. These boys have grown up to be big and strong. They are the strongest men in the village. Sunamite couldn't put her two hands together around their upper arms. Their muscles were that big. If big rocks needed to be moved near the river, these two would lift them with their bare hands. But they were ever so kind and gentle in dealing with people. They wouldn't harm an ant.

One day while they were fishing down at the big lake Runt, Sunamite's youngest brother who was the smallest of them all, took a small rock and crushed an ant that happened to be crawling by on the ground and Sonset asked Runt, "Why did you kill the ant? He wasn't bothering you. Don't take the little things life like that." Then tears started coming down Sonset's cheeks. Sonset tried to hide it but Runt told Sunamite later.

Sonrise and Sonset, at the age of 20, were strong as water buffalo. They would go down to the lake where the alligators were and grab them by the tail, wrestling them on the shore. They would take a piece of vine and tie the alligator's feet together.

Another day Sonrise, Sonset, and their father Razier were out in the jungle looking for a tree that they could make a canoe out of. As the tree that Sonrise was cutting began to fall, Razier tripped on a vine and one of the tree's large branches fell on his leg.
Sonrise and Sonset picked it up with their bare hands. Razier walked with a limp from that day onward.

Anna has been teaching Sunamite the English language. They spent many days under the Magnolia tree talking, reading, writing and telling stories about things that are happening in their lives. They developed a very close relationship.

On other days they'd meet at their favorite spot, down by the stream of water that emptied out into a large lake that was known for its large alligators. They had to be careful that they did not fall in. One day Sunamite and Anna were playing around, running through the jungle near the stream. Sunamite slipped and fell, rolling down the bank of the stream into the water. She hit her head hard on a rock and it knocked her out.

Though Sunamite was an excellent swimmer, she was now unconscious floating down the stream face down. Within seconds the water took her down stream, heading straight for the waterfall. Anna ran down a-long the side of the bank calling out, "Sunamite, Sunamite stop, stop, please stop. God please help her, please help her."

Then all of a sudden the stream took a quick turn where a tree branch was laying in the water. Sunamite floated up against the branch of the large tree. It was a Magnolia tree. It was the tree that Nolia and Sarah had planted years before Anna and Sunamite were born. The branch somehow had grown so low to the ground that it touched the water. It was one of the largest Magnolia trees Anna had ever seen. As Sunamite's body touched the tree's branches, she regained con-sciousness. She caught hold of the branch and held on. Then Anna climbed the other branches to get to her. She helped Sunamite to the bank. They lay there and cried for a while.

As Sunamite lay there in Anna's lap, she looked up and thanked God, then thanked Anna for saving her life. Sunamite said to Anna, "I will never forget what you have done for me. You are my friend forever." Sunamite got up slowly, looked down at Anna, smiled and walked over to the Magnolia tree. She reached up took one of its beautiful flowers. Then she walked back over to Anna handed her the flowers and said, "Friends forever."

They walked back to the village down the near path singing the new song that they had made up. It went like this:

"*Thank you God for making the big Magnolia so strong, So true, it helped Saved my dear friend so strong so true, Though streams of water tried to take Her away from me, the long arm of the Magnolia reached to the depth to bring her back to me. Oh, Magnolia, so strong, so true, we will always sit under your cover as "friends forever, friends forever, friends forever."*

After resting for a while they started down the path leading to the village. As they reached the village, Sunamite and Anna's father was waiting for them. Mr. Trader had to get back home. The girls told them what had happened to them. Razier said, "We will have a feast because my daughter could have drowned, but my Sunamite lives." He went on to say, "In three days we will have a feast because my daughter lives."

It proved to be one the biggest festivals the village has ever seen. All of the nearby villages came. There was a lot of music from the drums. Food was everywhere! Anna and her father came back to the festival. Everybody was enjoying themselves.

It was night time, the drums was getting a little too loud for Anna. She walked away from the village just enough so her ears could cool down a little. Just a little quietness meant so much at this time.

By this time Sunamite had missed Anna. She looked all over the village for Anna, with no result. Sunamite walked a little way down the path that lead to the river. This is the path they always take. Then she heard a scream.

"Help, help, please help me somebody." Sunamite ran as fast as she could toward the screams. It was Anna being attacked by a West African green Mamba snake. These snakes are long, thin, and highly venomous. They are capable of navigating through trees swiftly and gracefully. It will also descend to ground level to pursue prey such as rodents and other small mammals. She was up in the large Magnolia tree swinging a small limb at the snake. Sunamite picked up a good-sized stone and threw it as hard as she could. It hit its mark, right on the snake's big head. The snake retreated into the water. Sunamite helped Anna down.

Anna smiled, looked up, thanked God, and then thanked Sunamite for saving her life. Anna reached up in the Magnolia tree, picked one of its many flowers, gave it to Sunamite and said, "Friends forever." Anna hada yellow ribbon that her mother had given her tied around her waist. She took it off and gave it to Sunamite to always remember her as her friend for saving her life.

This they kept a secret.

22

Chapter 4

Teo and the Storm

Three months later Sunamite was sitting under the small Magnolia tree near her village. She was looking up in the sky. She always liked to look at the clouds, the many shapes they would have. Some would look like rabbits running across the sky. Others looked like people's faces, birds, mountains, fishes and many other things.

Then from a distance her eyes caught sight of a young man walking toward her. It was Teo. Teo is one of the village sons. An honest hard working young man, very respectful of older people. He would help the elderly by giving them some of the food he would kill in the jungle. Teo was a humble, quiet young man. Sunamite was glad to see him.

Teo's father walked up just about the same time as ask did Teo. Teo and his father were talking earlier about asking Sunamite's dad for her hand in marriage. Teo wanted to ask himself, so he did. He had asked Sunamite's father many times before, but Razier answer was always "No". Teo walk slowly with his head held high and his crest out, lowing his voice and said, "Razier, may I have your Sunamite as my wife?" Now this time it was, "Not yet." Teo felt he was making improvement. Teo didn't know that the two fathers had already decided it is too soon for them to get married this young.

Teo had brought her back a beautiful stone he found in one of the caves on his way back from his trip. He was thinking maybe Razier would say yes time. He had to sleep in caves at times so the lions wouldn't eat him for lunch. Teo spent hours filing the stone down to bring out the beauty in it. Yes, it was a gold nugget. Teo shaped the piece to make a necklace. He also took a piece of hide from a lion that he killed on his way to find his brother hunting, and made a necklace for Sunamite. Teo walk over to Sunamite and place the necklace of Sunamite head so gently, as she bowed her head. She started dancing all around the yard, running around and around the hut she lived in. Teo ran her down and grabbed her hand to stop her.

Many may say how could Teo, being so young kill a lion by himself? Remember David as a young man in the Bible killed a lion and a bear with God's help. (1 Samuel 17:37) God can help us do many things if we believe. (Please don't try that today)

Teo also was an excellent swimmer like Sunamite. He would put a knife in his mouth, dive to the bottom of the stream hold on to a rock and wait for a fish to come by. Then he would stab them with the knife. In the ocean he would dive for oysters and clams, sometimes getting pearls for his mother and sisters. They were so happy.

When he saw Sunamite smile he would start doing cartwheels.

Sunamite loved Teo very much, but she would respect her father's wishes.

Nolia, Razier wife and Sumamite mother liked Teo. She wanted a good husband for her daughter. Like all mother, would like a good husband or wife for their children. Nolia is a wife that was always seeing how things were going on in the family. Many nights she would lie awake praying that things would go good for her family. She would rise early every morning to prepare food with the other village women. It truly was a community setting in those days. People really cared about one another wellbeing. The Chief of the village kept things under control also. The chief son liked Sunamite also. His name was Loman. (L (o)-man) His name is of Irish origin meaning "small bare one". An Irishman visited this village earlier and befriended the Chief, so the Chief named his son after him. He did all he could to get Sunamite for his son. Sunamite didn't like him because she could look down in the top of his head. He was shorter than Sunamite.

Earlier Loman tried to get his father to offer Sunamite's father 100 head of cattle and 50 goats, but her father would always refuse. Razier, Sunamite father "said all the cattle and goats in Africa cannot buy my Sunamite."

Teo knew how to play the drums and flute. Sometimes during the late afternoon he would play the drums so that Sunamite could hear him play.

When she heard them she would think about the days when she and Teo would have their own hut. She hoped one day to have children that she could teach things to like her mother had taught her.

Early the next morning Sunamite awoke from sleep to help her mother and the other women of the village prepare breakfast for the villagers. These early mornings proved to be a good time to talk with her mother about things that were on her mind. By this time her father and brothers as well as some other village men had gone hunting. On their return they would no doubt be ready to eat.

As the sun rose above the trees it proved to be a wonderful day. The sun rise was just beautiful. It felt good just to see another day. Sunamite looked up to thank God for the gift of life itself. She remembered some of the things that Anna had read to her from the Bible. The skies were unusually clear that day. Runt had been talking to Teo and Sunamite about taking the canoe out in the ocean to go fishing and diving. All three agreed. Not too far from their fishing and diving, Sonrise and Sonset were helping their mother Nolia load the larger boat for a trip they had planned for months now to visit a village down the coast. Dry wood was gathered just in case they needed to make fire. This trip was planned for some time. Nolia will get a chance to see her mother whom she hadn't seen for a 2 years.

It would take them about a day's journey. Razier and some of his other sons had taken some goods over to Mr. Trader to sell. Razier looked up at the sky and it suddenly turned dark and the wind started blowing strong. All that he could think about is his family at the ocean shore.

Razier remembered Sunamite was going fishing and diving. They were a little of from the shore near some rocks. The wind blew harder and harder. He recalled the skies looked the same when Mr. Trader and Sarah had been washed up on shore a number of years back.

Razier and Mr. Trader looked at one another and knew something was about to happen. Razier, concerned for his children's safety, asked Mr. Trader would he keep his children with him and Anna. Razier and his oldest son ran as fast as they could to reach the shore. Razier couldn't run to fast because of his limp from the tree accident.

Sad to say Sarah, Anna's mother died a few months earlier from a bite from a very poisonous snake, the West African green Mamba. It was the same snake the attacked Anna earlier. This left Mr. Trader to care for Anna alone.

As the waves in the ocean kept picking up, getting higher and higher, Nolia cried out, "my children, my children, somebody help us." Nolia ran over to her sons, Sonrise and Sonset, telling them to get her children. But they couldn't swim. Nolia climbed up on the large boat and told her sons to push the boat into the water. They always listened to their mother. Sonrise and Sonset used every muscle in their bodies as they grunted and pushed the boat into the water. They were not going to let their mother go by herself, so they jumped in also.

By the time Nolia reached Sunamite, Teo, and Runt, their canoe was about to sink. The wind was blowing so hard. Sonrise and Sonset helped them on board the larger boat. Exhausted and tired, they lay on the floor of the larger boat. Now, what was Nolia going to do? The wind blew harder and harder.

The men tried to bring the boat to shore but the wind carried the boat farther and farther out to sea. The boat that Nolia was on had a sail also. The sail wouldn't come all the way down. In a matter of minutes the boat was out miles in the sea. The wind blew Nolia's hairpiece off. It was the hairpiece that Razier made from the lion's mane, the lion he saved Nolia from days before they were married. Yes Razier is a brave man. He would do anything to protect his Nolia, yes even from lions.

Razier's son reached the waters edge first, then Razier limped up just to see the top of the large boat carried farther out to sea until it disappeared from sight. He cried out in a loud voice "Nolia, Nolia, where are you? Nolia, Nolia, Where are you?" then he cried, "My children, my children, where are you?"

His oldest son Baako, the first born child, helped him from the beach shore because the storm had continually increased in strength. They took cover in a rock mass near the shore for at least 7 hours before the hurricane winds subsided. They watch as the sun set into the ocean. No more light for that day only darkness. Razier and his son, and Mr. Trader, Anna and the rest of the people came down to the shore to evaluate the damage. Everyone was in tears. Mr. Trader had to walk a few steps away for a moment because it brought back so many memories about his wife Sarah. What was going through Mr. Trader's mind? We can only imagine. Anna waited for a few minutes then walked over to her father, putting her arms around him and said, "Daddy, it's going to be all right." The light from the torches lit up the beach all night hoping that they would come back.

There were so many stars in the sky that night, more than usual. Prayers went up to God that night. Anna had been teaching the villagers about God from the Bible. It was the Bible her mother had given her.

Anna began think about her close friend Sunamite. She cried out, "Sunamite, Sunamite, where are you?

Sunamite, Sunamite, where are you? I will come and find you Sunamite my friend forever," cried out Anna again.

It proved to be a sad time in the village. They comforted Anna also, but all knew they must go on. Maybe in a day or so they would come back. Yes there is always hope.

The next day Razier, his oldest son, Anna and Mr. Trader used one of the other boats to sail out and see if they could find some sign of his family. About three miles out Razier spotted something in the water. It was the hairpiece that he had made from the lion's mane. But there was no other sign of them.

The hurricane had taken the boat hundreds of miles out into the Atlantic Ocean, far from the coast of Africa.

Sonrise and Sonse fought all night to keep the boat from sinking. They manage to get the sail down in time before it turned over. It was daylight now. Everyone was tired from the night's ordeal. Sunamite woke up crying, "Nolia I want to go home now." Nolia kept saying "Its gonna be all right Sunamite." Sunamite said, "My daddy will come and get me." He always came to her aid when she was in trouble. Then she said, "If my daddy is unable to come, for sure my friend forever Anna will come." Then the tears started to run down her face.

Hours went by, and then days went by. No one knew what direction to sail this large boat. All they could see was blue water everywhere. Runt started to get sea sick from being in the water for so long. Nolia took Runt into her arms and comforted him. They had enough food and water on the boat to last them for about seven days and nights. All they could do was drift. When it rained Sonset got coconut shells to collect the rainwater to drink later. Seven days had gone by with no help and no land in sight. What were they to do?

Birds flew by but out of arrow range. Teo was ready with this arrow, if he could just get a short. Late one evening a flock of birds flew low over the boat and some landed on the topsails for a moment's rest. Just enough time for quick-thinking Teo to use his sling shot and not the arrows. He was really good with his sling short. Teo trembling hands quickly place the one stone in the sling but it dropped out of the sling falling to the floor of the boat. Half of the dozen or so birds flow away. Teo slowly stooped down and pick up the stone, slowly rising again. He reached back and slung the stone with every muscle in his body, as if this could be the last chance for his last meal. His stone hit the target. Two large birds fell when the stone struck both of them. The stone was thrown so hard it traveled up in the sky after hitting the birds for about a minute than it fell back into the boat hitting the floor of the boat causing a small leak. Teo said, "Oops". He looked over at Nolia. She just smiled and quickly ripped part of her dress and plugged the hole. She reached for the birds and started preparing them to be cleaned and cooked.

They used a flat rock to cook on. They also used the wood that was on the boat for trip they was about to take earlier. Nolia could cook almost anything. A flint rock was used to start the fire. At night it would get cold, so this fire kept them warm.

Nolia was very concerned for her children and Teo, but it looked like there was nothing she could do.

She didn't want to show it. At night she would cry silently so no one could hear her. Runt knew his mother was crying a lot so he would go over and encourage her. "Nolia, we're going to make it," he would say with a hug. Then the tears would start to come again. Runt, a young man with a big heart.

The heat of the day was unbearable. It could drain all the energy that they had.

Sonset took some of the bird's feathers and made fishing lures and started catching fish. Teo had Sonrise, the strongest one of the twins, tie a rope around his wrist and lowered him down to the surface as he speared the fish that came to Sonset's lures.

Water ran out on the 12th day. Now what were they going to do? The boat kept on drifting who knows where. Late one night as they burned the wood, Teo with his keen eyesight and sense of hearing, couldn't help but   hearing something that sounded like people were having a tribal dance. He woke everyone up. They were so glad to get help.

Nolia was cautious about the ship they saw. Sonrise and Sonset were ready to protect all on their boat. But they had no choice. They took some torches and waved them back and forth. Sumamite took her necklace off and put the gold piece in her mouth.

Then they heard the men on the ship say, "Hello, hello, who goes there?" Sonrise replied, "We need help."

The men on the ship sent out two small boats and helped them onboard. The four men rowed the boats back over to the ship. The men helped all of them up to the deck of the ship. As Sunamite looked around she couldn't help but notice wine bottles all over the deck of the ship. The men were just drinking a lot of

31

wine, having a good time. Then she looked over to the other side of the ship and saw a Magnolia tree in a large pot of soil. The tree was about seven feet tall. She walked over to it and took one of its largest leaves. Then the captain of the ship said, "You like that tree, don't you. It's my personal tree; you can keep that leaf but don't touch it any more. Men have been shot for taking leaves off it."

This ship was a ship of friendly men. It was heading to the Carolina's to pick up cotton and deliver cloth. By now they were low on food. The captain wasn't going to turn the ship around and head for Africa. They were just thankful to be alive. It was going to take about 10 more days to reach South Carolina.

The captain of the ship was a good man. His name was Mr. Crib. There were no women on board. He gave the order that if anyone bothered any of these women, he would have them thrown over board. Then just two days later one man tried the captain out. This man made an advance at Sunamite. She was very attractive young lady. But the captain meant what he said and the man was thrown overboard.

The ship kept making squeaky sounds as it made its way across the waters.

Sunamite picked up one of the empty, clear wine bottles that were still on the deck of the ship. She went over to an area of the ship where no one was watching and took the Magnolia leaf out and scratched on the back of it the letters "TO S.C." and below that "SSSNRT O.K." Then she put the leaf into the bottle, poured a little water in the bottle to keep the leaf green and sealed it up with an old wine cork. She knew that the leaf was an evergreen one and that it would last a long time. Sunamite then threw it in the ocean, hoping Anna or any of the others would get it.

One day a man died from a sickness and they threw him overboard. This made Sunamite very sad. Nolia said to Sunamite, "Don't ever give up Sunamite, it's going to be all right."

One moonless night an even larger ship pulled up next to their ship. There were cannons all around it. It was pirate ship. The pirates got on the ship with out any fight. The pirates were looking for silver and gold. They found a small amount on the ship. As they were about to leave the ship one man said, "We need a good cook too." Finding where the women were, they took Sunamite. Then Nolia said, "I am a better cook. Take me instead of her." The man reasoned, well if he took two, he wouldn't have enough food. He took Nolia. Sunamite felt so alone, although her brothers and Teo were still on the ship somewhere. This ship just sailed away in to the darkness as sudden as it had appeared.

Her mother was gone in the darkness of the night. What was she to do now? "Nolia, Nolia, where are you?" cried Sunamite quietly. Then the tears started again. "What am I going to do without my Nolia?" she wondered.

Early one morning, one of the men said, "Land, we made it." She said to herself, "But made it where?"

"Charleston South Carolina," called out one man. She could understand some English because Anna had taught her a little.

Sunamite kept thinking on what her mother told her "not to give up!"

Chapter 5

Their New Home

Finally they made it to Charleston, South Carolina. By this time slavery was outlawed. People were free. But times were bad for the rich and poor.

When they decked the ship the first thing Sunamite noticed was all of those bales of cotton. And over there, Sunamite saw a beautiful Magnolia tree just like the one she and Anna sat around in Africa. But now, what were they to do? No money. No parents. Nowhere to lay their heads for the night. No food. Now they are in a strange land. Her mother Nolia's words kept going though her head, "Don't give up Sunamite, it's gonna be alright."

By that time Mr. Crib walked up and asked them all, "Where are you gonna go? Each one looked at the other and Sonset said, "We'll have to make it somehow." Mr. Crib said, "I see you are strong men, I lost some 10 men on my journey here from England. I could use some help in getting this cargo off here. It would be about 10 days work for all of you. And the young girl, can she cook?" Then all of a sudden Sunamite smiled and Teo saw it and started doing cartwheels again. Mr. Crib said, "I know you're happy to get a job but you don't have to do all of that!"

They worked for 20 days and lived on the boat until those days were up. They had made some money to take care of some of their expenses. Mr. Crib had Sonrise and Sonset go with him into town and he would bet on their weight lifting ability. He made a lot of money on them.

Teo could dive deep into the waters. The men of the city would throw silver coins into the water and Teo, with his keen sight and diving skills, would dive to get the coins. As time went by Mr. Crib offered them a trip back to England. They told him since his ship wasn't going to Africa they would have to find another way home. Mr. Crib said he had a relative coming down from Magnolia, South Carolina. (Later to be named Lynchburg) so they should see him before he set sail. He would be glad to talk to his relative to see if he could help Sunamite and the rest of them. The group readily agreed.

The next day Mr. Crib's relative came down to Charleston with some cotton for the mills. His name was Mr. Chase. They were first cousins, two sister's children. Mr. Chase agreed to hire all of them. Mr. Chase looked at all five of them, Sonrise, Sonset, Runt, Teo and Sunamite. Mr. Chase said to Sonrise, "Can she cook?" Sunamite spoke up quickly, "I have a mouth of my own. I can speak for myself. Yes, I can cook, clean, sew, knit, wash clothes, and more. Yes, my mother taught me all these things." Mr. Chase said

"That's what I like. Someone that can speak their own mind."

They traveled along the dusty roads that lead to Magnolia. She couldn't help but notice the Magnolia trees. Again she thought about Anna. Would she come for them? Yes, Magnolia, Magnolia where are you? She looked for the tree with the yellow ribbon on it. At this time she said, "Anna is coming one day."

Finally they arrived in Magnolia, South Carolina. The year was bout 1880. Sunamite was exhausted from the long wagon trip from Charleston. Mr. Chase had a large plantation. There were houses, sitting off from the main road, big and tall. Sunamite wondered, "could people live in that?" She noticed that it was a little different than the other houses in that area. Most houses only had one story. Big white poles were in the front. She counted four poles. All around the house were smaller buildings. There were hogs, cows, horses, mules, dogs, cats, chickens, and ducks all over this large farm. The fields that surround the house went on forever. Sunamite, Teo and her brothers had never seen so much flat land.

As she looked around from one side to the other, she saw Magnolia trees. They had green leaves on them all the time. That made her wonder again, "Where was Anna?" Would she ever come and get them? Magnolia, Magnolia where are you?

A man showed them where they would be staying. A woman in the house that did most of the cooking was introduced to Sunamite. "Hi, my name is Flossie what's yours," said Ms. Flossie. That's the name Mr. Chase gave her. "My name is Sunamite," replied Sunamite.

Then from around the corner of the building, came Mr. Chase, out of nowhere he showed up asking Sunamite, "what is your name?" She said, "Sunamite, what's your name?" No one said anything. Ms. Flossie asked, "Can I give you a nickname?" "What's a nickname?" asked Sunamite. "It's a name that a person would call another person instead of this real name, but it wouldn't change his real name." Sunamite agreed. Ms. Flossie said, "It be Ebony!" Now Ebony turned looked at Mr. Chase and said "Your nickname will be Mr. Cotton because of the white hair on your head." Mr. Chase just walked away shaking his head.

From that moment Ms. Flossie and Sunamite developed a close relationship.

Ms. Flossie could cook some biscuits! Well, about anything she wanted to cook, she could do it. Ebony learned more about cooking from Ms. Flossie than she had learned from her own mother. Sometimes Ebony would sneak and cook some African dishes for Ms. Flossie. Mr. Chase didn't want to waste his food. He didn't like some African's foods. They had many conversations together. Ms. Flossie could tell you many stories about her life in Africa and here in South Carolina also. Ms. Flossie was here for over 2 years now. Ms. Flossie eyes lit up when she talked to Ebony about her wedding day in Africa. Ms. Flossie recalled how handsome and strong her husband was on their wedding day 15 years ago. Her father had a big feast for them. All the villagers were there. They danced into the late hours. Everyone put on their best outfits they could make. A good time it proved to be for all.

Ms. Flossie's husband was killed by nearby villagers that attacked their village late one night. She said, "He was a brave warrior. We didn't have any children before they killed him. I loved him so much. His name was Nest. Yeah, like a bird in his nest." The tears started running down her face. Ebony just hugged her and cried along with her.

Chapter 6

The Land We Left Behind

Back in Africa Anna was still at lost because her best friend was gone. Five years had passed, to Anna it seem like forever. Most had given up hope of ever seeing Sunamite, Teo, Runt, Nolia, Sonrise and Sonset again. But something inside Anna was still holding on to seeing Sunamite, her "friend forever," again.

Early one morning Anna was walking along the beach. Now that Sunamite and the others were missing she would do this every morning. All of a sudden she stepped on something that hurt her foot. She dug down in the sand and pulled out a bottle with a leaf inside of it. She looked through the clear bottle to try and see what it was but moisture prevented her from seeing clearly. She carefully pulled out the cork and saw that it was a leaf. Anna took a small stick from the ground and fished the leaf out.

There was something scratched on the Magnolia tree leaf. It had "TO S.C." and below that "SSSNRT O.K." It was a message from Sunamite! Anna started jumping up and down saying, "They are alive, they are alive in South Carolina." The message meant "To South Carolina, Sunamite, Sonrise, Sonset, Nolia, Runt, Teo." Yes, she knew it was from Sunamite because it was on a Magnilia leaf. Anna quickly ran and told her father and Sunamite's family.

By this time Anna's life had changed. There was a mining group that came to this part of Africa looking for gold. Mr. Trader let them dig on his property. Yes they found gold, a large mine. This must have been where Teo got the gold that he made Sunamite's necklace from. He did not know it was a gold mine.

This group had been mining there for about two years now. One of the young men that were working in the mine fell in love with Anna. They were married shortly thereafter. Soon they had a little girl. Anna named her Carolina Sunamite Moses.

Not too many months later an unknown virus broke out in that area of the jungle. It affected over half of the people in the villages. Anna and her husband used some of the money from the gold to construct a small hospital to help the people. Some doctors were brought in from other towns many miles away.

Shortly afterward her daughter came down with the virus. This delayed there trip for a number of months, but she eventually recovered.

Anna was very dedicated to this cause of finding Sunamite. She knew that she had to go and find her friend and the rest of them. Her husband, Mr. Moses, agreed. Anna's father and Razier agreed to send Mr.

Moses, Anna and their daughter Carolina, while they took care of the hospital and the mining. They didn't waste any time. The next ship was leaving in 10 days, they would be on it.

Back in Magnolia (Lynchburg, S.C.) Runt asked for a meeting of the whole group to come together and talk about what were going to do. They had been there in Magnolia for about five years and hadn't set any goals for themselves. Runt said, "We have worked and haven't saved anything. We have no plan on how we're gonna get back home." He asked for suggestions.

Sonrise said, "We can work and give Ebony the money to save for us. Yes, she can be our banker." Everyone agreed.

"We must seek ways to make money so we can get home," said Teo. "We need to send Ebony to school too, so she can keep up with what's going on around us."

Ebony smiled and said, "That sounds good. I would like to learn more about nursing. I like taking care of people." Then Ebony smiled.

After Teo stopped doing his cartwheels they continued with their meeting. Sonset said, "It was good that Mr. Chase let us build our own house on his land and sharecrop to make some money. But we only seem to be able to pay off the bills we made the winter before. We are just breaking even," said Runt, "We'll raise hogs, chicken, grow a large garden, and make baskets, until we make enough money to pay our way back home."

Again everyone agreed. Now they had a plan.

Ebony was able to enroll in the one-room school in a town of Magnolia. She learned English, arithmetic, and writing. She was so happy. They were saving money now. Ebony was secretly hiding the money at the root of a big Magnolia tree at their newly built house. She did that because Runt always wanted to borrow money. This was the money they were going to use to get back home. Things were looking up. She wished that Anna could be there to share her newly found knowledge as a nurse.

Chapter 7

Ebony Abducted

Every thing was going well for about six months; then things changed again.

One day Teo and Ebony had a big disagreement. Teo didn't live in the same house with Ebony and her brothers. Her father wouldn't have anything like that in Africa. Ebony, although thousands of miles from home, kept her father's wishes. Teo had agreed to take Ebony to town that Saturday evening, but he played kickball with her brothers instead. When she came to tell him about it he was talking to Ms. Flossie's neice who had come to visit. This upset Ebony so much that she ran away from home. This was not a wise decision. She went down the road until she reached Lynches River. She walked down under a bridge that crosses the river. This was about two miles from her house. That river is still named that up until this day.

Wagons were always coming across the bridge. She realized that this wasn't a wise place to hide, so she started up the riverbank. As she reached the road a wagon came a long on its way toward Magnolia. Two men were on it. One man asked, "Where are you going?"

"Home," said Ebony.

"Where is home?" asked the other man.

She said, "Africa!"

They started laughing at her. She continued walking and the men continued riding along beside her.

"Go away, go away you men" Ebony retorted angrily.

One man said, "We're just kidding, get on the back of the wagon and we'll take you as far as Magnolia." It was dark by now. She agreed and sat on the back of the wagon. Anyway, one of the men looked a little like Teo.

The men were steadily talking to one another low enough that Ebony couldn't hear what they were saying. About a mile into the trip one man said to Ebony, "We're almost there, would you like a watermelon to take home with you?"

She turned her head around and smiled and said, "Thanks you sir." She was a little hungry by now.

The man lifted the canvas that covered the small watermelon slowly. Higher and higher he lifted it. Then he quickly threw it over Ebony. She could hardly breathe.

She screamed, "Let me go, let me go you animals."

The other man had joined him by that time. They put something over her mouth and tied her hands and feet. One man said to the other, "If we don't harm her she'll be worth more money."

"You're right," replied the other man.

When they got to Magnolia, it was completely dark. There were three men walking in their direction. They drove by them with the mules at a steady run.

Sonset hollered out, "Have you seen a girl down by the river. Have you?"

"No," both of the men replied. The mules continued running.

When the three of them arrived at Lynches River, they could tell that Ebony had been there. All three of them were excellent at reading trails.

Teo couldn't help but wonder where was Ebony? He cried out, "Ebony, Ebony, where are you? Ebony, Ebony, where are you?" He knew she was an excellent swimmer. She loved life too much to commit suicide.

They couldn't figure out what happened. All of their money was gone also. Taking their torches, they started on their way back to Magnolia. They planned to come back the next day to look again when they could see well.

The two men reached a town called Mayesville about one hour later with Ebony. Then they turned right and traveled about one more mile. The men stopped the wagon, whispered something to each other, and then continued. The men had reached the house, but to make it seem to Ebony that it was a long way off from her home they kept driving the wagon up and down the road for three more hours. She noticed the wagon came to a stop. She just knew she was far from her house.

There was a third voice now. "Good job boys." It was the man of the house, Mr. Smith.

The two men were looking for a young girl that owed Mr. Smith some money. She had agreed to work for him until it was paid off. The only thing is it wasn't Ebony. This young girl just looked like Ebony to Mr. Smith. When they pulled the cover off Ebony and untied her she explained that it wasn't her.

Mr. Smith didn't have good eyesight any way. He said, "It's you all right." So she had to stay there. Mr. Smith's house was off the road a little. It had rows of trees in its front yard. One tree near the house was a Magnolia tree. From the road you could also see a large oak tree.

Months went by and Ebony was trying to figure out how she could get away form there. In the meantime, as she helped in the house, things started happening. It was about noon one hot summer day. Mr. Smith had just come in from the fields, keeping a watch on how things were going. He had a man that told him everything that happened on the farm. He got a lot of people in trouble for telling on them. Mr. Smith named him Hash because he liked to eat hog hash. Every evening Hash would report to Mr. Smith on what the other farm hands were doing and saying. After a while the farm hands got to know who to trust and who not to trust.

But this day Ebony was the only woman in the house cooking. Mrs. Smith had gone to town to get some food supplies. Mr. Smith washed his hands. Then he looked over at Ebony with a crazy smile. She felt very uncomfortable. She had never seen him acted that way towards her. He walked over to her and said, "Honey girl, you know I have lots of money. If you would be my second wife I will give you some of the money."

Ebony strongly replied, "If you come next to me I'll cut your head off. I will have a husband one day. I will fight you until I die before I would let you touch me," said Ebony. Mr. Smith said, "I can hang you for talking to me that way, you know."

"I would rather die," Ebony angrily replied.

"You owe me, you know," said Mr. Smith.

"You might think I owe you, but my heart is not for sale," said angered Ebony. He never approached her that way again.

Chapter 8

Reunited

Months had gone by in Magnolia and still no Ebony. The young men had gone through a lot in their lifetime. Runt kept telling all of them, "Remember what Nolia always told Ebony, 'never to give up.' We must keep on going."

As soon as those words came out of Runt's month Teo looked over Runt's head and said, "There's somebody coming down the road."

"We don't see anyone coming, you're playing one of your tricks again," Runt said. Teo had good eyesight.

A wagon was coming with a man and woman on it, also a little girl. Sonrise, Sonset, Teo and Runt were sitting on their front porch; it was about 7 o'clock in the morning, just turning daylight. The people reached Mr. Chase's house first. He met the people in his front yard. They talked a while, than laughed awhile, looking over at the young men. What was going on, wondered Runt? The people and Mr. Chase started walking over toward the young men. They all had smiles on there faces.

The woman called, "Sonet, Sonrise, Runt, and Teo it's Anna! Anna from Africa, I came to find you."

They all picked her up and hugged her. They did their African dance in the yard until dust was everywhere. Yes even the men cried.

Then things got quiet. Anna, still crying, looked around and asked, where is Sunamite?"

The young men looked at one another and Runt said, "We don't know." Runt explained what happened, then Anna's tears of joy turned into tears of sadness. Runt reminded everyone again, "We must not give up hope."

Anna and her family rested up a while. She told them about how their mother Nolia was all right. She was in Africa. More dust started flying up.

Anna had an uncle just a few miles outside of Mayesville that they were to meet in 3 days a 3 o'clock for dinner. Anna had written him months earlier. She had to be there by that time because he was planning on taking a trip to Atlanta, Georgia late that day if she didn't show up. She had three more days to get to Mayesville.

Now three days later, in Mayesville, Mr. Smith's wife Bell was preparing a meal for her quests. Ebony noticed this day seemed to be different. The sky was clear and blue. The air smelled so clean. There was no smell of hog pens. The birds seemed to be happier that morning.

At about 3 o'clock in the afternoon, Ebony was about her cleaning again on the front porch. She glance over at the Magnolia tree in front of the house and wondered to herself, "Is Anna coming?" She put her hand into her apron and there was a yellow ribbon that she was saving to put on the Magnolia tree when she got a chance. She looked around to see if anyone was watching. All was clear. She ran off the porch over to the other side of the Magnolia tree. She tied the yellow ribbon on a limb of the tree so that if Anna came up to the house she could see it on that side of the tree.

This Magnolia tree was taller than the two-story house. Its limbs touched the ground under it. Ebony got into the habit of sneaking Mrs. Smith's Bible out of the house and climbing up in the middle of the tree where no one could see her. She couldn't hide in the oak tree like she could in the Magnolia tree. She would read the Bible as often as she could. She remembered the passage in the book of Genesis, at chapter 1 & 2, where it talked about how Adam and Eve were in Paradise. They didn't have any cares at all. Ebony kept picturing that one day she and Teo could live like that. The closest thing to paradise she could remember was back home in Africa.

As soon as she got back on the porch she could hear something coming down the long dusty road. Yes, more visitors, thought Ebony. So she ran back into the house to let Mrs. Smith know someone was coming.

Mrs. Smith said, "I am expecting visitors from overseas. So, hurry and get things ready. Hattie was another young lady that had gotten herself into debt so she had to work to pay if off. Ebony said to herself, "overseas, where is that?"

Now they hurried and got the stove heated up even more. The wood stove had never failed them. It was 100 degrees outside while they were cooking in the kitchen.

Mrs. Smith met the guests outside after their long hot dusty ride on the wagon. The stable man took the horse and wagon to the stable for water and hay. They were white people, a man a woman and a little girl, Ebony observed as she peeped through the curtain. As they came up the steps Ebony ran back to the kitchen to continue preparing the food.

"Girl, you're gonna get caught doing that one of these days," said Hattie.

As they entered the door Mrs. Smith gave her guests a drink of fresh water that she always kept near the front door on these hot summer days. By the time Mr. Smith had entered the house from the back door. He changed his boots and washed his hands and dried them, then headed for the dining room where the quests were seated. They greeted one another and continue talking. Ebony didn't hear their names.

Ebony couldn't help but hear the laughter. She knew she hadn't seen them before. She asked Hattie, "Who are those people?" "They are from Africa," said Hattie. "I am from Africa too," said Ebony. But no one paid her any attention.

At that moment Ebony thought about Teo. If only she could smile for him right now. Tears ran down her cheeks.

Then Mrs. Smith said, "Hattie, you can bring the food out now."

"Yes mam, Mrs. Smith," replied Hattie.

Ebony got the pot of rice and took it in first. As she opened the door she got a good look at the man and his daughter who were seated across the table from her. The woman's back was to her so she couldn't get a look at her face. Ebony left the room to get another dish.

Ebony asked Hattie if she could take the green beans in next. "Sure, why not," said Hattie with a puzzled look on her face. When Ebony entered the room she went around to the other side of the table to get a look at the woman. As the woman looked up from eating her food, her eyes and Ebony's locked. This woman had the bluest eyes you would want to see. Just like Anna's eyes.

Ebony quickly left the room thinking, I've seen those eyes before. They look like Ann's blue eyes. Her heart was almost beating out of her chest.

Ms. Hattie looked over at her and said, "Have you just seen a ghost?" Ebony couldn't say anything at first. She was breathing too hard.

The little girl, who was seven years old, didn't want to eat her green beans. Then all of a sudden Ebony heard the mother said, "Carolina Sunamite Moses if you don't eat your green beans you won't get any dessert."

Then Anna asked Mrs. Smith, "Who tied the yellow ribbon on the Magnolia tree out front?"

"I don't know, Ann, the wind must have blown it up there," said Mrs. Smith. Ebony left the kitchen slowly, moving toward the dinning room with tears in her eyes.

Standing near the door with a smile on her face, she said in warm voice, "Magnolia, Magnolia, where are you?"

Anna stood up from the table with tears in her eyes, turning and said, "Here I am Sunamite, my friend forever."

They ran across the room toward each other and hugged and cried.

Everyone at the table was wondering what was going on. Then Anna's husband remembered her telling him about Sunamite. That's why they gave their

Daughter the middle name, Sunamite, to remember Sunamite.

Ebony said to Anna, "My nick name is Ebony." Ebony and Anna were jumping all around the room just like little girls again. They stopped long enough to tell everyone what was going on.

At that time it was revealed that Mr. Smith was Anna's uncle, her father's brother. Anna told her uncle and aunt all about how she had known Ebony in Africa. How Anna's father and mother were heading to Jerusalem and the ship sank in a hurricane off the Africa coast. Only her father and mother survived that trip. They stayed in Africa for a number of years then went on to Jerusalem. They liked Africa so much that they returned to make it their home.

Anna said, "Later, I was born." One year later her mother was hanging out clothes on the line when a poisonous snake bit her on the leg. She never recovered from the snakebite. That's why Anna became so attached to Sunamite, because she didn't have any sisters or brothers. Her father took her everywhere he went.

Anna now told what happened to her all those years since Sunamite and her family was taken away to South Carolina by the storm. By this time Anna and Ebony had taken a seat at the table with the others. Mr. Smith looked over at his wife, then back at Ebony and Anna. No one made any move to stand up. The point was understood.

Anna said she learned the next day what had happen. But the day of the storm, her father came home with little to say. He usually tell Anna about his day. He just went to his room and sat in his favorite chair. Anna said she questioned him, but he said "Anna I just don't feel like talking right now." She said she just left him alone for the rest of the day.

"The day your father and older brother came over to trade some goods with my father, I was finishing up painting a Magnolia flower on a coffee cup for you. Then the wind got up all of a sudden. There wasn't time to do anything."

Anna asked, "Where is your mother, Nolia?"

"I wish I knew," said Ebony. "Mother was taken from us at sea." She paused a moment to catch her breath. She was crying again.

"We were on the boat for weeks then a ship came by and picked us up. While we were on this ship a big black pirate ship came along. These men were looking for gold and silver. These pirates wanted someone to cook for them. They had guns and long knives. The men on the ship didn't put up any resistance.

"If my father had been there he would have protected us," said Ebony angrily. Those pirates made all the women come up from below.

One of the pirates said, "Take the young dark one," said Ebony. But Nolia spoke up and said, "I can cook better then she can, take me instead." So, they took my only Nolia. That's the last time I saw my Nolia," cried Ebony.

Anna talked about how Mr. Moses came to Africa in search of gold. Her father let him mine on his land. At first there there wasn't any gold to be found but Mr. Moses never gave up.

"We were married with my fathers blessing shortly after the gold mining began," Anna said.

"Then the next year Mr. Moses found gold on our property. A lot of it! Although we were rich, I wasn't happy knowing what had happened to Sunamite and her family. I told my husband we must find them, even if it takes forever. Then I found the bottle you sent on the beach shore," said Anna.

"You got it?" smile Ebony happily.

"Yes I did! Then I knew we had to come."

Ebony laughingly recalled one day when her brothers Sonrise and Sonset were plowing with the mules on 10 acres of land, getting it ready for the cotton to be planted. Sonrise couldn't seem to get one of the mules to listen to him. Sonset had no problem with his mule Minnie. He was laughing at Sonrise and his mule Sadie.

Sonrise said to the mule, "You're gonna listen to me." Sonrise stopped the mule in the middle of the field, unhitched him from the plow, walked around to the front of the mule, grabbed him by this front legs and threw him down on the ground like a man. When the mule got up he had no more trouble with him.

Chapter 9

Freedom

Anna asked, "Ebony, do you want to go home now?"
Mr. Smith spoke up and said, "I know you are my
niece and everything, but I just can' let my help go just
like that. She owes me a lot of money."

Ebony explained that there was a big mix-up. "Mr.
Smith thinks I am someone else. Those two men
brought me here from down by the river near the city
of Magnolia," Ebony said with a strong voice.

"Wait a minute," said Anna

She pointed to the small table over in the corner
and asked her daughter Carolina, "How about handing
me my purse over there in the corner please?" When
she picked up the purse it was kind of heavy for
Carolina, but she managed to get it over to her mother.
Anna reached inside and handed Ebony the coffee cup
that she had saved all these years for her. The
Magnolia flower on it was still beautiful. Mr. Smith
looked kind of puzzled.

Thinking that she was going to hand him a coffee
cup, he began shaking his head from side to side.

Anna reached back into her bag and pulled out a solid gold bar about six inches long, two inches wide and one and a half inches tall. The gold bar had "99.9" written on them. Then she asked her uncle, "Is this enough?" He shook hi head yes.

"She is free to go," said Mr. Smith.

Anna reached into her bag again and pulled out some thing that looked like a pine cone. She said, "This is one of the seeds that came from under the large Magnolia tree in Africa. I was keeping if for Ebony also.

Ebony said, "I will plant it in my front yard when I get my first house in Africa."

Anna agreed. They laughed then walked out on the front porch and sat in the rocking chairs to continue their conversation.

Early the next morning Ebony and Anna were up packing Ebony things. Hattie was in the kitchen cooking bacon, eggs, grits and her golden brown biscuits. Ebony told Hattie she would come back to see her.

But Hattie said, "No you won't, I'll be coming to see you and your brothers." They just laughed.

On the way back to the town of Magnolia Ebony said "Let's surprise my brothers. Let's tell them Mr. Smith gave you a hog. It is on the back of the wagon under the cover, but I will get under there." That's what they did.

When they reached Magnolia the four young men were busy building this new house that Anna didn't tell Ebony about. This was the house for the four men to live in. Teo was on top of the house putting on roofing. The other three were working on the outer walls. The three of them had learned many trades over the years.

Runt was the bookworm by now. He could read a book in one day. As a matter of fact he was writing a book about their life story but didn't want to finish it until he found out what happened to Ebony.

Sonrise was the best blacksmith in the area. People would come from all over to get him to work on their horses and mules.

Sonset grew the best crops in town, cotton, corn and beans.

Teo cooked the best barbecue in town. He learned that from his father back in Africa. His father would cook meats over the hot coals.

As Mr. Moses stopped the wagon in the yard, he asked the three men if they would help unload this hog that Mr. Smith gave them to barbecue. Runt came running first. "Oh how I love barbecue," san Rant. All three reached for the cover about the same time.

Then Ebony rose up, pulled the cover off her and said "It's me, Ebony."

They were beside themselves with joy. The dust filled the yard from all the dancing, and hugging. The joy they felt could not be described.

Then they heard a noise from on top of the house. "What's going on down there?" asked Teo.

Sonset said, "We've got a hog to barbecue, come on down and see.

Teo climbed down the ladder and walked cautiously Toward the wagon, thinking this was another one of their tricks. The dust was still thick. He walked straight up to Ebony and paused.

She smiled. Teo did a cartwheel. Then he picked her up in his arms and tenderly kissed her. They made more dust fly.

The three brothers said, "This will be Teo's and your house, we will build us another one."

Ebony interrupted and said, "Anna has told me about conditions in Africa. Many people are sick there. I have learned much about nursing so I want to go back and help my people."

Teo spoke up and said, "Not without me!" He walked over to her, looked her in the eyes and asked her, **"Will you be my wife?"**

She smiled, and said, **"Yes, my Teo."**

He kissed her and started doing cartwheels all over the yard. It took Sonset, Sonrise and Runt to run him down.

Ebony then walked over to the large Magnolia tree, took a stick, and began digging. This was where she had put the money for the family.

She said, "Here are the silver dollars I have been saving for us to go back home one day. Now Sonrise and Sonset, you can keep it. We'll just use enough to get back home."

Anna said, "No, give it all to them and also these gold bars." She had two large gold bars.

Carolina had learned how to play the flute from Anna. She reached down into her little purse that she always carried around on her arm. She pulled out her little flute that her father had made for her. All of them had remembered the song that Anna taught them. This was the song that Ebony and Anna had made up together back in Africa. While Carolina played the flute all of the rest of them sang, including Ebony, because she remembered it also. She taught it to her brothers and Teo. Yes, she would sing it to herself at Mr. Smith's house.

It went like this:

"Thank you God for making the big Magnolia so strong, so true, it helped Saved my dear friend so strong so true, Though streams of water tried to take her Away from me, the long arm of the Magnolia reached to the depth to bring her back to me. Oh, Magnolia, so strong, so true, we will always sit under your cover as 'friends forever, friends forever, friends forever.'"

They spent the rest of the evening talking.

Anna and her husband sent funds to Africa so all her other brothers, sister and her father could come to the wedding.

Three days before the wedding Ebony and Teo were still making preparation. Carolina was outside playing with her puppy. Everywhere Carolina went he would be there. Carolina looked up and saw a lot of dust down the dirt road. She ran over to the barn and told her father.

It was a man riding a horse, coming down this long dusty road. The Moses family didn't live in the town limits of Magnolia. They lived about three miles out west of town. They were hoping this was Ebony's family.

It was Mr. Brad, the town's policeman. Mr. Moses greeted him and offered him a drink of water. Mr. Brad said, "No thank you Moses, I am here on business."

"What's the business?" asked Mr. Moses. "There are some people in town saying that they are from Africa. They want to know where you live." "One said his name is Razier.

"They are here," screamed out Mr. Moses to the rest of the family! "They are the relatives of the people that lives in the house over there," pointing to Teo's house. "Where in town are they?" asked Mr. Moses.

"By the stagecoach stop," said Mr. Brad. Mr. Brad got on his horse; he said that he would keep them at the stop until Mr. Moses get there.

By this time everyone was running out of the house to see what the screaming was all about. Mr. Moses told everyone that Ebony's family was here. Again the dust started to flying all over the yard. Mr. Moses suggested that he and Anna better go to town together to keep down confusion. Everyone agreed.

When Mr. Moses and Anna arrived they were told that some of Ebony's sisters and brothers didn't have the right papers. This was going to cost some money.

Ebony's father Razier motioned and said, "I will pay. How much?"

But Anna asked Mr. Brad, "How much does it cost?

"Over $300 dollars," he said. Anna reached in her pocketbook and pulled out a small gold bar and handed it to Mr. Brad, and said, "Is this enough?"

"Plenty, plenty, they can go. You all have a nice day."

As the three wagons made their way out of town there were many songs sung in the African tongue. These were songs of joy.

When the wagons were approaching the house Ebony and her brothers and Teo were standing at the edge of the yard jumping for joy. Some of Ebony's brothers jumped off the wagon and ran ahead of it reaching Ebony and the others with big hugs. More dust was flying up all over the yard. Everyone was crying. Razier looked up and just thank God for letting him see all of his children again.

When the tears cooled down a little, Ebony, holding her father around the waist, said "If only Nolia could be here." They had not told Ebony about her mother yet.

At that moment the cover on the wagon pulled back and a voice said, "Here I am."

It was Ebony's mother Nolia. Ebony ran over to the wagon and helped her mother down. Words can't explain the joy these two had at that moment.

Nolia then told them about how the pirates ran low on food after so many days and had to land off the coast of West Africa. One evening they took her to the waters edge to help find food for them to eat. Nolia was very familiar with the plants in that area so she gathered some plants that, if eaten, would put you to sleep.

After boarding the ship she made a big tasty meal. The men were walking around rubbing their stomach. The other hostages were not allowed to eat this meal because it was so good. In 30 minutes all of the men were asleep. Nolia told how she and all of the hostages got in one of the boats and headed for the shore. She knew the area, so eventually she made it back to her village.

Yes, this proved to be a family reunion. Sonrise was walking around holding one of his younger sisters up in the air over his head. He was so glad to see her again.

Now it is time for the day Ebony and Teo waited for so long, to be together as husband and wife. These two had gone through so much as young adults. But they never lose sight of what was right and wrong. They wanted their marriage to be an honorable one be for God. Ebony read her bible almost every day. She had to remind Teo many times what it said.

Planning for the wedding was so much fun for Ebony and Anna. They decided to make Ebony's wedding cake. They said they would call it a Magnolia cake. Runt had to put two round cake pan together to make one pan. It almost looked like a large number eight.

Ebony also made Carolina some Magnolia cookies. They also looked like the number eight but smaller. "They are so sweet," said Carolina.

Ebony and Teo had a beautiful wedding. Ebony wore a beautiful white dress that reached the floor. When she walked it looked like she was walking on the clouds of the heavens. When the birds flew by they would stop and look at her from the nearby trees. Her hair was so long that it reached down to the middle of her back. Teo dressed in his black suite. A slender handsome young man. He was so in love with his Ebony. Anna was her maid of honor.

Shortly after the wedding, Ebony kept her word. She and her husband returned with Anna and her family to Africa to continue the work that Anna had started. The rest of Ebony's family returned to Africa also. Teo and Ebony built a house in sight of the beautiful waterfall. They would sit on their back porch in the evening and watch the waterfall together. The sound of the water rumbling, and the fresh air that it presented was just out of this world. They were glad to be back home.

Runt went back and found himself a wife. Not the chief's daughter, whom he could have married, but sweet humble beautiful young lady. She had beautiful teeth. What impressed him so much about her was what when he came courting she would prepare the fire from wood she had gone in to the jungle to get herself. She would carry the wood on the top of her head while in her hand she had other pieces of wood.

Sonrise and Sonset stayed in Magnolia. Sonrise married Flossie and Sonset married Hattie. Both couples had a set of twins each! Ten months later Teo and Ebony had twin girls. They named them Mag and Nolia. One was named after her grand mother.

The question still remains, "Magnolia, Magnolia, where are you?"

Why? Who are they today?

Part 2

A Sharecroppers Family

**A Lynchburg Sharecropper's Family
1930s-1960s**

Next I'm going to tell you a true story about a Sharecropper's family from South Carolina. Today many children don't even know what the word sharecropper means.

This group that we are looking at is from the era of the early 1930s to 1960s in a rural South.

Yes, sharecroppers had an agreement with the owners of land that they would work the fields (cotton, corn, tobacco, wheat, oats, and other crops) to produce crops that when harvested, the income would be divided by the landowner and the sharecropper.

The landowner provided the house the sharecroppers lived in. These houses usually had no running water. There were outdoor toilets with no running water as well. We would have to move these toilets when the hole we dug in the ground was filled with human waste. Sometimes these toilets had two seats in them.

The life of a sharecropper, the man of the house was the one who worked hard to provide for his family. A lot depended upon how hard he and his family worked that year. He had to pay for all the bills the family made doing the winter months. He would have to borrow from the landowner to buy food, clothing, and medical expenses, during the winter months. A lot rested on the shoulders of the father. He was a man who would work from sunup to sundown, earlier and later than many others, as we will see.

As for the children, we had our responsibilities. We had chores to carry out also. We would cut wood to make fires in the fireplaces or put it in a heat that burns wood, so that we could keep warm during the winter months. We picked cotton, cropped tobacco, fed the hogs, took out the cow, and brought her in at the end of the day. We had to hoe the yard of all the grass, cook string tobacco, baby-sit the little children, bring in water for the night, wash clothes, and plow the fields with mules, not tractors. Hoeing the yard free of all the grass, down to the dusk, was needed because back then we didn't have lawnmowers.

Now let's talk about the mother in the family. Besides taking care of the children, she worked in the fields alongside her husband. She cooked, washed clothes, canned food for the winter, and scrubbed the floors of the house. Sometimes the floors were wooden.

You could see the chickens and dogs walking under the house at times. Most of the time she also took care of the little financing that had to be done-light bills, if they had lights, furniture bills. And she had to discipline the children most of the time.

We have always been able to learn from the past. How have other families survived over the years.

This groups of people have almost been forgotten – the sharecropper's families. But for most of us from the United States in the southern states, these are our grandparents, great grandparents or great, great grandparents. Take a moment in your life and ask, and you might be surprise at the information and stories you can find out about them.

Mothers were usually the backbone of the sharecropper family. I would refer to them as Magnolias but when we were children we never called anybody Magnolias. Not to say that they were not call that by others. Sometime the name Southern Bells would be heard. They were strong physically and mentally, just like the literal Magnolia tree. Magnolias are beautiful. The pretty flowers are on the tree during late spring and early summer.

One word that describes, my mother Violar M. Green, is LOVING. Not to be over looked, there were and are many, many more strong women on this vast earth.

There are mothers who are during all they can to provide for their families. Many single parents are caring the load all alone. There is a Bible scripture that can help: Ecclesiastes 4:9, 10 "Two are better than one because they have a good reward for their hard work. For if one of them falls, the other can help his partner up. But what will happen to the one who

67

falls with no one to help him up?" Our hearts goes out to you. It is difficult enough when there are two parent in the household. If single fathers step up, knowing that your child is your flesh and blood. Don't leave your child behind. This world is to dangers, even for us adults.

Some of the things Mom did for us, her 12 children, had to be put in writing. No she wasn't perfect, but surely loving and caring for her 12 children, not to mention the many grandchildren, as well as other children in the community. She was like a mother to them. Other children would come over and Mom would set a plate of food on the table for them too.

Violar, is third of eight children born to Rev. Jake and Julia Carter. Julia Carter, my loving Grandmother, had such a big heart. I was very close to her. She was so humble.

I remembered when I would stay the night at my grandparents' house, she would cook those biscuits that would melt in your mouth. The fresh ham out of the smokehouse out back. (The smokehouse was were my granddaddy would store hams from the hogs he killed earlier) Oh those grits and eggs, they were so good. I still love grits and eggs today. The coffee my grandmother made, I can't find anyone to make it taste the way she made it. She made covers for the beds with her hands taking pieces of cloth and sewing them getter. (See one on my web site) All grandmother children and grandchildren loved her. We missed her so much.

Granddaddy or Papa we would call him was short in statue (about 5' 1", I took after him) but no less of a man. When he spoke we listen. A hard work man. He had his on land that he farmed. He had mules that he worked his fields with. No tractors, he couldn't afford them. But as time passed he became a sharecropper. Maybe I will tell you that story one day. But sometime its best not said. This book couldn't hold all the things I enjoy around my grandparents.

My mother, Jake and Julia's daughter was married to Frazier Green on November 8, 1931. He is the father of all 12 of us. He was strong, humble, caring, educated, quiet man that stood over 6 feet tall. He loved his children very much.

Their wedding was performed at St. Matthew A.M.E. Church. The reception was under a large pecan tree in Lynchburg, S.C. This six-foot, nine inch man fell in love with the five foot, four inch lovely lady. He was from Manning S.C.

They said that of all my grandparent's children and grandchildren, I am the only one that looks and acts like my grandfather Jake.

After Frazier and Violar married they moved in with his brother, the Rev. Green. This wasn't far from Violar's parents. They stayed there for about a year then decided to move in with Violar's parents. During that time they had their first child, Shirley Mae Green.

After staying there for about a year they decided to get their own place where they could raise their children. My dad met a man name Frank. He owned a number of acres of land closer to the city of Lynchburg. Yes, Lynchburg was a thriving little town at that time. In the mid 1930s passenger trains would stop at the Lynchburg Depot. There was Lesane fish market, they had the best fish sandwiches in town. These sandwiches tasted so good. (The fish restaurant is Timmonsville, SC, at the light, today reminds me of Ms. Lesane fish market – restaurant). In Lynchburg there was a Post Office, drug store, doctor's office, hat store, clothes store, cotton gin house, not to mention a bank, a finance company, and baseball fields as well as a large mule stable. Dad used to walk to the stable early every morning Monday through Friday to get the mules to work in the fields, then bring them back every evening after finishing the work for the day. He would then walk back home about two miles each day.

Shirley recalled a time when Freddie Mae, her sister, and her were in the bed playing together with their doll babies. Dad was nodding (sleeping) in front of the fireplace. His head would go up and down, side to side as he slept. Shirley and Freddie Mae would say "Look at that head going back and forth, back and forth." Then they would laugh.

Then all of a sudden Daddy got up out of the chair, acting like he was going into another room. As he walked by the bed he reached over and started pinching them. Daddy was just play with them. He love us so much. Daddy's pinches were so powerful that he pinched them with the cover still over them and they felt it. They hollered and called Mom, and Mom would say, "See there you all shouldn't be picking at Frazier." When he finished they said it felt like they were stinging all over. Daddy's pinches would stay with you for quite some time. Daddy would almost never disciple us, Mom took care of discipline.

Shirley said she remembered the times when she and Mama use to go up town to the hat store (I can't remember the store name) on Main Street, which is now Magnolia Street, to buy hats and other items.

There were two little ladies that owned this store. There were times when Freddie and Shirley would go together. One day Shirley and Freddie were on their

70

way back from the store when Mr. Frank drove by and stopped, asking them would they like a ride to their house. They accepted but they rode on the outside of the car. This car had a running board that you could stand on. They held door handles, Shirley on one side of the car and Freddie on the other side.

Shirley recalled the times when Mama would say, if you didn't go to church you couldn't have any boy friends over.

When they had homework for school they would go to Daddy. He seemed to always have the answers. Daddy was a very educated man. He went to school in Wilson South Carolina near the city of Manning. He had the chance to becoming a teacher.

Shirley even recalled when they didn't have lights, but lamps fueled by kerosene. If for some reason a person had to go to the kitchen you just had to sit in the dark until that person got back. "Sometime we used fat light sticks to see by," said Shirley.

Shirley couldn't forget what Mama went through having all those children. She recalled the midwives, Ms. Rosa, Ms. Cook and Mrs. Ester. They were the ones that would come to the house and deliver the babies. They would send the children out of the house.

Midwives delivered eight of Mama's children. A doctor in Lynchburg delivered the other four children. After Mama had the baby, she would stay in the house for one whole month. She wouldn't go outside at all. She would close the curtains and would read, with no light at all.

Grandmother would come over and help her during this time. Also Aunt Addie Bell from Lynchburg and Aunt Sally from Manning would come and stay about a month to help.

Then there were the boys that came over courting. Mama would allow it but she had to be sitting in the doorway while they were there. When time came for them to leave, Mama would start clearing her throat.

Freddie Mae would go to school all nice and clean, but return home with her hair all messed up, clothes torn off her. She would get into fights at school all the time. Shirley and Freddie would be dressed down in their black and white shoes and their wide tail dresses.

When Shirley and Freddie were younger, they said around Christmas time they would get gifts. But they could never catch Mama and Daddy playing Santa Claus. When they woke up on Christmas morning the stockings would be full of candy by the fireplace.

Now if you want to know stories about the family just talk to Freddie Mae. What a memory she have.

Addie came along, the third child and third girl in the family. She was just a lovely person, easy going, quiet, mild type of a person. Do you know anyone like that? In many families there is usually one.

Now the house had three girls in it, no boys. One thing about our family is that we did things together. There wasn't much outside influence. A close-knit family is what it proved to be. We played together, sat in the evening and talked and laughed together.

If we had to leave the house for some task we had to perform, mother wouldn't completely rest until all of us were back home that evening. She didn't keep us in a closet either. We always had room to grow. She wanted us to learn new things in the world around us. She wanted us to learn new things, or in other words keeping up to date on matters of education and our surrounding. She did not want us to be looked down on by others, as if we didn't know anything. Her children were just as much as the next person's children. And she would let people know that too.

Addie was like a second mother to me. I first came to know a lot about her when I was able to visit Brooklyn, New York. Before Addie left the south she had a little girl, her name is Shirley Anne Greene.

A single mother parent leaving the south trying to make it better for herself and family. She left her daughter with Mom, who Shirley became like a sister to us.

Now there were times she would send for me to bring Ann to New York. I was about 10 years old when I got to take my first trip to New York. I was sitting on the front porch waiting for the man to come and pick us up. Yes, I must have sat on the porch all morning waiting for that man to come. Then there he was coming down that dirt road. The man that took Shirley Anne and myself, loved to smoke. On the road to New York, he was smoking a cigar. The smoke got into his eyes. It was so bad that he couldn't see how to drive, so his wife had him to pull over to wipe his eyes. I was afraid that we were going to wreck.

Cars, cars, trucks, trucks, for miles and miles that's all I could see. We would stop for a moment at rest areas, sometimes just pulling on the side of the road and run behind the trees for our restroom.

Yes, Mama cooked us plenty of fried chicken for the trip.

I was in for the shock of my life. The Big Apple! New York City proved to be as BIG as they say and even larger for me. How could they have built such tall buildings? The Empire State Building was the tallest of all at that time. Later Addie took us there, all the way to the top.

Now when we reached the streets of New York City people were everywhere!

"Where are they going?" I asked myself. Some of the people had briefcases, black hats and long black coats on.

On the streets, it looked like trash was everywhere. "I wanted to go back home," I said to myself. As we got to my sister's house, things seemed to be getting better. But there were a lot of people everywhere again.

My sister was a hard working person. (Magnolia) She was not the type that would lay out of work, calling in sick just because she had a little headache.

Addie would take us shopping, seemed like every other weekend. If not shopping, we would go visiting friends or family.

She worked in a watch factory for a number of years. She gave me a watch one year. Later I found out that this watch was made out of 18 karat gold. When it stopped working, I had it made into a necklace for my wife Desiree.

Now let's go back to Brooklyn. There were a lot of house parties back then. A lot of people would come over and dance and eat and drink and drink and drink. That was when I learned how to really dance.

This was in the early 1960s to the late 1970s. James Brown, Otis Redding, The Temptations, Marvin Gay, Mary Wells, Sam and Dave, Aretha Franklin, Wilson Pickett, The Miracles, The Four Tops, Al Green, as well as many, many more singers were popular. I could go on and on. My brother Sammie, (I'll talk about him more, later) really thought he could dance like James Brown, sliding across the floor all the time.

Addie had many house parties, but all of a sudden people started breaking into her house, taking many of her things. Shortly after that, house parties as I recalled started to cool off. We would now go to the clubs. Party!!!!!

The Fraizer and Violar had their first son **Robert**, in 1938. Up until now Daddy carried the weight of the farm mostly on his own. Daddy was fairly young at the time. Now Robert really began helping at the early age of eight or nine years old. He helped plowed fields of cotton, tobacco, corn and other crops. He remembered having to stay out of school for days just to work in the fields.

Robert said, "Our future brother-in-law Tom McClain.(He married Shirley the oldest sister) used to help Daddy with the fields also."

Robert recalls these words that were told to Daddy many times by the landowner, "You just came out even," or, "You just made it." This meant that the crops or the harvest that was sold for the year was just enough to cover the expense. "Many times we didn't have much money, but we never went hungry," said Robert.

There were peas, corn, flour, greens, chicken, hogs, milk (from a cow we owned), butter, eggs, corn meal, grits, and much, much more that we had on the farm.

Mama's chickens would produce so many eggs that she would sell the eggs to make extra money for the family.

Mr. Stukes had a ginning mill in the town of Lynchburg. People would bring their corn and he would grind it up into whatever you wanted it to be.

Yes, it hurt Mama so much to see all our hard work in the fields taken from us.

Daddy and Mama loved each other very much. They had this mutual respect for each other. Mama would get to Daddy sometimes. Daddy would never hit Mama, but there were times when he pincher her.

In 1941 another son was born, the fifth child. I don't remember very much about **Jake** because I was born in much later and Jake left for New York earlier.

Jake had asthma really bad. Sometimes Mama used to burn some kind of powder that would smoke and Jake would inhale it. Mama would always take care of her own children. Jake was a little on the bad side because he didn't have to work in the fields as much as the rest of us.

Jake left home after school, looking for a better life. When he got to New York he became a New Yorker. He liked nice things, clothing and housing. He was the best dressed out of all of us. He proved to be a hard worker in the jobs that he found in New York. He worked for the New York Transit Authority.

Now the sixth child, **Sammie,** recalled how Mama made sure all of us had breakfast before we went to school each morning. She cooked grits, eggs, bacon and those hot brown biscuits. Sammie was born in 1943 and he talked about those biscuits like he had some yesterday.

My daughter Tenell, born in 1984, tells me how much she misses those biscuits. "They would just melt in your mouth," said Tenell, now sixteen. She probably was the last person mother made them for, before she stopped cooking. Sammie talked about the greasy lunch bags he would carry to school each day.

There were times when Sammie and Daddy would go uptown (Lynchburg) to get the mules out of the "livery stable" where the mules were kept overnight.

But the problem here was that Sammie and the other boys always had a time in trying to catch the mules. See, you would have to put the harness around their heads. Sometimes we would chase the mules all over the stable and never catch them.

Then Daddy with his deep voice would walk up and say in a deep manly voice, "Come here Mennie or Sadie or Loddie," and the mules would come up to him with no problem. He had that much authority in his voice.

During the day we would plow the mules so much that they would sweat. On those hot days sweat would be poring off their back like someone poured water on them. When time came for them to use the bathroom, they would just stop right there and do so.

The mules also knew when it was time for lunch. Mr. Jones had a store in the town that had a whistle that he would blow at 12:00 each day. You could hear it for miles. We knew then it was time for lunch. We wouldn't have a watch in the fields, but mules knew it was time for lunch. They would stop in the middle of the field. They made some kind of noise to let you know it was time to loosen the plow so they could go home and get something to eat and drink. They would be blowing air out of their noses.

We had many good times with the mules. One day Robert, was driving the wagon with the mules pulling it down this long dirt road. He had Sammie and Joe (the brother next to Sammie) on the wagon also. He started making the mules run so fast that when they reached a curve in the road they couldn't stop. Sammie was thrown from the wagon, hitting his head on the wheel of the wagon. He didn't get hurt too badly. He still has the scars on his forehead today. Sammie was about 13 years old then. Mama took him to the doctor. Maybe it was that blow or hit that made Sammie think he could dance like James Brown.

There was a problem when it came time to go to school. The land owner said, "Those boys don't need to go to school." Mama would step in and say, "My children are going to school!"

The land owner would go to Daddy and say, "You've got to do something about that woman, Violar." Daddy was a little afraid that the owner was going to make us move off his place. Mama and Mr. Frank would have it out about her children going to school. But she stood firm that all of her children would be educated.

On Saturday mornings we would pick cotton, so we would have money to spend for Saturday night when we went to town. Sammie said "All I wanted to do was to beat Joe in picking the most cotton." He's the next child mentioned.

Joe could pick over 100 pound of cotton on Saturday mornings. I recalled how Joe and Mama would pick two rows of cotton at the same time. Some of you out there know what I'm talking about. They would pick one row up a few yards and then turn around and go down the other. On a full day of cotton picking Joe and Mama could pick over 400 pounds.

Sammie was good in sports. He played football, baseball, and basketball in high school. (Mt. Pleasant High, Elliott SC) He recalled some of his teammates like S. Wilson and H. Edwards.

Sammie graduated in 1963 and during that same year he left for New York. Again looking for a better life, he went looking for a good job.

Then **Joe**, came along in 1945. He helped a lot on the farm. Joe recalls Mr. C. Jefferson, a well educated man. He would spend a lot of time with his students.

Mr. Jefferson was a teacher at Mt. Pleasant High School in Elliott, South Carolina.

This was a man of many professions. The Mayor of Lynchburg, SC, a funeral home owner, later a principle of Bishopville School. He helped to get a lot of grants for the city of Lynchburg, including the water, sewer and drainage system. I remember when water would be in the streets so high that we could swim in the streets.

Joe was one of the best basketball players at Mt. Pleasant High. They won the State Championship in 1964. He received two trophies that year. One of them I am looking at now in Mama's house. The other trophy is in the High School trophy case. Mama didn't care for that idea too much. Joe recalls one of his basketball teammate, M. Yates of Sumter, SC. Joe also played football, and he was a tight end for his team.

Mama didn't want Joe to play football. She was thinking that he would get hurt. He sneaked and played anyway, signing Mama's name on the paper. But one day it became evident. He got hurt. I will never Forget Joe coming down the dirt road so exhausted, limping very badly. See Joe wanted to play football but Mama didn't want him too. She was afraid he would get hurt. He even signed mother name on the paper so he could play. We got hurt. He was in so much pain, Mama asked him, "Are you all right Joe?" He would say "yes mom," then turn his head and flinch his face. I think Mama knew.

Joe graduated high school in 1965. Then he left for New York.

Ruby was born in 1948. She was the eighth child and the fourth girl. She recalls on wash day how she would make fire around the big black wash pot to heat

79

the water to wash the clothes. They didn't have hot water heaters back then. Ruby and Mama taught her how to cook, clean, quilt, canning of vegetables, fruits and other items.

Oh, how I remember that you didn't go in the kitchen while Ruby was cooking. She would come out and sit down until you left the kitchen. We would be so hungry because of smelling those homemade biscuits.

Ruby recalls how Mama would tell Miss Bell (new landowner) off many times in the fields. Miss. Bell was Mr. Frank's older sister. She became the owner of the farm after his death.

There were many more people that helped us through these times, the 1960s and 1970s. A leader, Mr. T.R. Robinson in our town and in the church was willing to help many of the young people in this small town. He taught Ruby how to drive. He was a very patient man. He was the man that put the word in for me to get my job in the bank in 1973. The bank wrote him to ask about me. We often talked about this. I thanked him for all he did for the young people and me.

All of the help really came in good. If we can see how to help a child or young adult, it could start them on a new road in life. Showing a caring attitude for other may in these days save their life.

I was the first in the household during the 1960s to have a driver's license. Ruby was working in a nearby town named Florence. She didn't have her driver's license at the time, so I had to drive her to work every morning before I went to school. Mama would ride with us every morning. Mama made me slow down for every curve in the road. I thought she was asleep, but how wrong I was.

"Slow down Hubert," Mama would say. Ruby would be knocked out in the back seat.

It helped me to truly learn how to drive.

When I got to school that mornings, school wouldn't have started yet. Now by the time I get to my fourth period class, my English teacher, who spoke so softly, would put me to sleep. That's why my English isn't the best today.

Saturday was fish cleaning time. We would clean fish so that we could eat it for Sunday morning breakfast almost every Sunday.

Ruby recalls when we would walk barefoot down the dusty road on the way to church. Then right where the dirt road met the paved, Mama would take a damp cloth out and wipe our feet. Then we could put on our socks and shoes.

Now comes along something different. TWINS BOYS! John and James were in born 1950. They were Mama's bundles of joy. She never chose one child above another. She treated all of us alike. There were no favoritism she show toward her children.

John talked about how he would drink all his milk out of his bottle then find James to get his bottle. What John would do is make a distraction for James. John would find something for James to do so James would put down his bottle. While James was busy John would sneak back and get James bottle and drink all the milk. When James finally thought about his bottle, he would go back to find it empty. "Ah, Ah," James would bust out in tears running to Mama "Milk, milk gone", James would say. Mama thought James drank all of it.

John grew up to be taller, bigger and stronger than James. I wonder why? Mama did find out what was going on later. Not much got past Mama.

John also worked the fields just like the rest of us. He liked sports also. He always wanted to do what his older brothers did. Especially like his older brother Joe. He recalls the time when he had to take turns going to school because it was his day to plow the fields with Daddy.

John said he remembers the dog named Blackey also. Mama would leave Blackey with them at the end of the cotton rows while she picked cotton. No one would be able to come near us. One day a lady came working up toward the small children while Mama was up in the field picking cotton. Blackey ran after the woman almost tearing her dress off. The lady went running down the road until Mama came to her rescue. Blackey look out for us.

John knew how to make some money on Saturday morning. Mrs. Johns, the wife of a store owner in the town of Lynchburg let him work for around their house them.

James loved to eat cornbread when he was small. He would walk around the house with his cornbread in his hand for hours. The chickens would run after him because he would be dropping crumbs all over the yard.

James also recalls Mama didn't allow any alcoholic drinks in her house and no smoking was allowed around her children. Daddy and Mama did not smoke.

James mentions we didn't have softball like today. We didn't have softball like today. We had "softballs." They were big and soft. Now they are very hard.

There was this young boy from town. His nick name was Two Tom. He was strong!

I (Hubert) was the leader of the group from the farm. He was the leader of the group from the town. We got into a fight one day. I never knew a person could hit so hard. We became the best of friends later.

James recalls when we attended Fleming Elementary School in town. The principle would let us sell cookies for the school at lunch time to the students. We would get a hand full of cookies for doing this. Also we would stand in line to ask if we could wash the dishes in the school cafeteria.

Then we would get a free lunch. Yes those were the days.

Now to tell the story I recall about the early life around my mother and family. I **Hubert**, was born in 1951. It was a rich childhood for all of the children and grand children of Frazier and Violar. I just want to tell a few more things that I experienced around my mother (Magnolia) during my early life as a sharecropper's son.

I can think of things as far back as when I was five or six years old. When we ate breakfast or dinner we all had our own separate plate to eat out of. We got in wood for the house year round because Mama had to cook on her wood stove winter and summer.

My Daddy used to go shopping for the family every Saturday morning. Those Cracker Jacks he would bring us, would light up our day. Those boxes would have some great toys inside of them. I loved putting them together. Since there was so many of us, all of us couldn't go with Daddy on the wagon that the mules would pull. We had two mules that I remember very well. The first, high spirited one was named Sadie. And the slower, fat but so loving one was named Minnie. An easy going, easy to ride mule she was. But Sadie always wanted to do things her way.

There was a time when Sadie wanted to do things her way with Daddy. Now that wasn't going to work. Daddy was the man and he let the mules know that. One day Sadie tried Daddy's patience. Daddy loosened her from the plow. Then he pulled real hard on the ropes. Then he gave her the beating that made a mule respected him. Sadie would jump all around but Daddy would hold her with the rope. She behaved from that day forward. Sadie's eyes got so big when she got her whippings.

Poison Spray?

I recalled one day my brothers James and John and I were walking to the local city dump not far from our house. My brother John found a spray can. Being the kind of person he was, clowning around. He sprayed it in my face. I thought that it was bug spray, poison. I thought I was going to die. It seemed that I began having shortness of breath. All I could think of is that I was going to die. I look up to heaven praying and running as fast as I could all the way home. I had my hands held in the praying position, crying and praying, "Please God don't let me die." He didn't. John and James laughed at me all the way home. I told my mother, I think she laughed a little behind my back.

Trees

When we moved into our new house thing was so much better than the farm. It was like we were free. I went across the field from our new house and got two medium sided cedar trees, at two different times, put them in a pot of soil. After a period of time I planted the trees in the front yard. From the highway the cedar tree next to the light pole is the first one and the second one is next to the neighbor's fence. In the middle is the Magnolia tree my mother planted herself.

Killing Hog Day

Daddy would sharpen the knives that morning by rubbing them against a piece of stone. Daddy and Mama always had hogs for the family. We would have to feed them every morning, midday, and at early evening. Even after we moved into our new house we had hogs to take care of in the far back yard.

We would go with Daddy to see how he was going to kill the hog. We only had one gun in the house, a single shot shotgun. Daddy couldn't use that type of gun because it would mess the head of the hog too much. Mama had to make hog head cheese out of it later. That was the best hog head cheese that anyone could eat.

So Daddy would use the ax. He would put some corn near the edge of the hog pen. Daddy was so tall he would reach over and swing the ax and hit the hog in the front of this head with the back of the ax. Then

Daddy would take his small knife and cut under the hog's neck so the hog could bleed. Then we would hurriedly care the hog near the house where very hot water was ready in a barrel. We dip the whole hog in the barrel of hot water then pull it out with knives in our hand ready to scrap the hair of the whole hog. We didn't want to keep him in the hot water to long because it would burn the skin. Most skin was to be cooked later as crackling or pork skins. After a number of dips and scraps the hog would be clean and hairless to be cut open down the stomach.

Daddy was go at this, you almost had to be sergeant to care this out. Daddy have skills. He would start the first cut with the flesh opening quickly from the pressure of the large hog. See if he cut to deep the knife could hit the intestines. If that happen it could spoil all the meat.

After cutting the hog open and taking out all its organs Daddy would take him down and place him on the large table so that he could cut him up in pieces. He would save some skin off the hog for cooking pork skins. The small intestine would be cleaned by Mama and my sisters. What was a bad smell? Then he would take other parts of the hog and grind it up and put it into the small intestine to make sausage. You're talking about some good sausage!

Mama would salt down the hams then hang them up in the smoke house for us to eat later. She would send me to the smoke house in the morning to get cuts of meat for breakfast.

Mama would always share with her sisters and brothers and our grandparents and others.

Taking Care of Business

Each time Mama got out her pocketbook it was time for business. She knew how to deal with anyone. It didn't matter whether they were rich poor, black, white or red. Mama could handle business matters. Buying things for the house when she had the money was no problem. I noticed that she would not get into a lot of debt. She taught me many things about business. Maybe that's why I have been working in business field for over 40 years now and still at it. When I was about 9 or 10 she would tell me about things she wanted to buy. She would save her money under the bed mattress until she had enough to buy what she wanted. If only we could save money the way she did.

Playing Golf

There was a man that came out to the farm to play golf every once in a while. He would go down the dirt road and get out of his car with his golf clubs and balls. He would start hitting golf balls all over the fields and woods. I wondered why he wasted all those balls! He would get in his car and just leave all those balls everywhere. We would go across the fields and get as many balls as we could find, then come home, get a few sticks, dig a few holes in the ground and start playing golf ourselves.

Rolling Tires

There were times we would go to the city dump down from our house. We would get old tires that were thrown away. We would get in a line and race the tires by pushing them with our hands. John always seemed to win the races.

Bang of a Time (1961)

There was one time my Uncle John visited our house at night. This was my Mama's youngest brother. He had had a few drinks. He and I were standing outside talking for a while. He reached into his pocket one between his pocket to get a cigarette, pulled one out of his pocket, putting one between his lips, and lit it then, BANG! It was a firecracker that he had put in his mouth. It busted his lips and blood was everywhere. Mama always came to his rescue. Mama would do all she could for her kid brother. He called her by her nickname, "Sister".

Leaning How to Drive Manually (1962)

Uncle John had a light green Ford that I loved to drive by the time I was about 9 years old. I would be glad when he came by. We would sit down and talk a lot. He would spend a lot of time with me, because I would listen to a lot of what he told me. It would be good if children today would spend more time with older people instead of just there on age. They could learn things that would help them later in life.

When Uncle John was ready to go home, he would ask Mama if I could go with him. When we got a little ways down the dirt road he would stop the car and get out, and let me drive.

This was a manually operated car. It would choke off a few times but he kept telling me, "keep trying." Then all of a sudden the car would take off. The gears would scrape a few times but we were on our way.

Mustang Sally (1965)

I had a classmate whose father bought him a 1965 Ford Mustang. It was fast! We would go over 100 miles per her hour in 60 seconds. (Don't try this) He would start the car up, back it up, and then all of a sudden he would put it in the first gear, releasing the clutch. The car would just sit there and spin for a few seconds and then take of the other way. WOW!

Hurricane Hugo

In 1989 when Hurricane Hugo came to South Carolina it hit Lynchburg hard! It happen on a Thursday night. I was watching the track of the storm for some days now on the Weather channel. The weatherman reported how it came off the African West Coast. I was at work that Thursday morning listening to the weather reports on how it was heading straight for the South Carolina coast. Around 4 pm, the winds began picking up.

I knew I needed to get home to start taping up the windows and taking some other safety steps such as removing any lose things in the yard that could be air borne. After leaving work at around 5:30 pm, I headed straight for home. The winds increased more and more. The clouds had that look of a hurricane sky. I remembered the look of the skies during other hurricanes.

We decided to fill the bathtubs, sinks, buckets, and anything that could hold water.

We put important books and papers in large trash bags just in case the house was destroyed, these things wouldn't get wet. We got in our car and drove it up to Mama's house, parking it at the back door. This was about 8:00 pm. The wind was getting worse. No one really knew how bad it was going to be.

Mama didn't have Alzheimer's disease at this time. She was glad that we came over and stayed with her. She was there alone. It hurt me to see her there by herself, there was nothing I could do at that time.

Many times on my way to work I would stop by and see how she was doing. (She live across the field from me, on the same road) She would say, "I never thought that I would be living by myself after raising 12 head of children and 3 grandchildren. At this time all but four, (Hubert, Joe, Viola and Ruby) had moved away to New York and Maryland.

Being just a good mother and grandmother, Mama also babysat Ruby's two daughters for her as well as my daughter Tenell.

She was not used to cooking just for herself. I wonder could this have added to or brought on the Alzheimer's disease, her spending so much time alone, after spending so much time around all those people.

The later it go that night the worse the winds blew. The lights went out. That is when I knew it was close. I had this battery-operated radio that we were listening to. The reports from down in Charleston weren't good. There were all kinds of reports of buildings damaged, trees down power outages and on and on.

The eye of the storm came just 20 miles west of us and hit the town of Sumter SC hard. People were calling this radio station in Sumter all night long with stories of how trees had fallen on their cars and houses. Some were crying, asking for help. This radio station was operating by a gas generator by the way. The station sent one man out in the storm and he almost didn't make it back. Power lines were down everywhere.

Now about 12:01am Friday morning, the winds got to be troublesome. I tried looking outside: you just couldn't see anything it was so dark. The tress at the windows were almost laying down, the wind was blowing so hard. They would blow one way for a while then they would lean the other way because of the changing of the wind direction. I will never forget that howling sound of the wind.

By this time we were all in the middle of the house, in the hallway, down on blankets and pillows. It seemed as if the roof was going to come off. People were still calling in to the radio station, "The wind just blew out my windows," said one woman.

All of a sudden we heard a big thump. "What was that?" asked my wife Desiree. I really didn't want to go and see, but being the man of the house, I got up slowly and peeped out the window. A large tree in the neighbor's yard had fallen and hit our pecan tree and in turn, it fell in our yard. The neighbor's tree was over 100 years old. Its trunk must have been over 10 feet across. I think that was the night for prayer. Many were sent up all across South Carolina. (If so let me know on my blog at magnoliawork.net)

While talking to a lady in the store a few days later she said "I had never heard my husband pray before, but that night he put down some praying."

Mama's Magnolia tree kept standing. The pecan tree had fallen just next to it. The Magnolia tree just lost a few leaves. I recalled when my brother and sisters would come home from New York they would get small branches with leaves on them off the tree. I asked them why they were doing that. They said it would help them keep money. When I visited them in New York they would have the branches in the corner of their rooms all dried up.

Yes, daybreak told the story. Trees were down everywhere. I had a small mobile home across the field behind my house that I was going to rent to my cousin in about a week; I had already turned the lights on.

The wind picked that mobile home up and threw it about 25 yards from its original spot up against some trees. The body of the trailer was separated from the floor of the trailer.

Mama's house didn't experience much damage, just a few shingles blown off the top of the house. Some of them hit my car that was parked in the back yard. My house had a tin top and tin around the bottom. That was most of the damage I received. We didn't have power for about two weeks. The water in the bathtubs came in good.

We couldn't drink the city water then either. My Aunt Addie Bell Commander (Mom sister) still kept her hand pump. That came in good for drinking water. I remember carrying some water to an elderly lady in plastic bags. She appreciated that so much. She would tell a lot of people about that kind deed that was done to her. We got aide from outside sources also.

Yes, we survived Hugo! (What hurricane you survived?)

Now the 12th and last child **Viola** born in 1954, I will let Viola tell you her story:

You would thing that being the last of 12 children a mother's love would be getting a little thin, but to the contrary, my Mom's love very strong for me. This strong force of love between us is what I miss so during Mom's sickness. When Mom's illness caused her to forget me and say certain things, I didn't think I would get through it, but with God's help and strength, here I am today. (Mom was diagnosed with Alzheimer disease)

I remember having an illness at a very early age that caused my hands, arms and legs to breakout. Certain times when it really got bad it would cause my eyes to swell shut. I can remember times not being able to see but hearing my mother's voice talking and praying for me. A lasting memory from my childhood is hearing mother praying that God would bless her and let her see her children grown up to be able to care for themselves.

Funny how, this is my prayer today.

Mom believed in keeping us healthy. See, there were three older brothers, one older sister and a young nephew and niece I mostly remember growing up with.

I can remember at the beginning of the winter we had to line up and take a large spoon of Cod Liver Oil and some orange juice one at a time. I never wanted to be the first.

That lining up wasn't always for medication. There were so many of us so that when something was done to cause us to get punished, Mom would have one go out and get a switch from a certain bush and we would have to line up and one by one get our punishment. I did not go first! My nephew Larry Green would always run and have to get his last. He died as this book was being written in 2001. We always called him by his nickname, Mickey.

We didn't have much, Mom made sure we ate and kept us clean clothes.

Another line: we would all get at least one pair of shoes for Christmas, so after opening our gifts we would use our shoe boxes, get in line and get fruits, candy and nuts from Mom. Now this had to last us until New Years. We would get more (in line again) on New Years Day.

Mom's love is like the supernatural spirit; even if she didn't speak it, you felt a strong love, just unexplainable deep within love.

Mom had a strong mind for business. She was always working things out for her family. She would do housework, just making $25.00 a week and spend $25:00 of it to feed her family for a week.

After my father passed away Mom was determined she would not marry again, and she never did remarried.

One day Mom told me to make sure that I keep the family home available for my brother James to live in it if he needed to come home from New York. Since he didn't have a wife, she wanted me to agree that I would see to it that he had a place to live. So now, as I get older, I am making sure my daughter keeps Grand Mom's request.

Part 3

Conclusion

So, Magnolia, Magnolia, Where are you?

Some would like to know what has happened to my mother. She died at the age of 93. We miss her so, so very much. We hope to see Mom and Daddy again soon. Yes by means of God's kingdom we hope to see many of our relatives back in the resurrection of the dead.

It have been a joy in writing these books and other works mention below. I must say the greatest joy of all is coming to know my heavenly father Jehovah God. There is so much wisdom mention in his word the bible. My favorite web site is JW.Org.

If Mama was here today, she would still give her sons and daughters good advice. I think it would go something like this from the Bible book of Proverbs.

At the 31st chapter verse 1 it states like this:

1. The words of King Lemuel, the Prophecy that his mother taught Him.

2. What, my son: And what, the son of my womb? And what, the son of my vows?
3. Give not thy strength unto women, nor thy ways to that which destroyeth kings.

4. It is not for kings, O Lemuel, it is not for kings to drink wine; nor for princes strong drink:
5. Lest they drink, and forget the law, and pervert the judgment of any of the afflicted.
6. Give strong drink unto him that is ready to perish, and wine unto those that be of heavy hearts.

28. Her children arise up, and call her blessed; her husband also, and he praiseth her.
31. Give her of the fruit of her hands, and let her own works praise her in the gates.

Well, could big things come from small beginnings?

Well from this small book came:
- 3 other books
- 1 Stage play
- 100 page screenplay
- could be more.....

Thank you

The End

Made in the USA
Las Vegas, NV
13 November 2021